WHISPERS

WHISPERS

Dereck and Beverly Joubert

HYPERION BOOKS FOR CHILDREN

New York

For information address Hyperion Books for Children,
114 Fifth Avenue, New York, New York 10011-5690.

Printed in Singapore

First Edition

1 3 5 7 9 10 8 6 4 2

This book is set in 18-point Berkeley Book.
Library of Congress Catalog Card Number 98-86794
ISBN: 0-7868-0454-8

WHISPERS

It was a hot, dusty day when the baby elephant was born.

He recognized his mother by the sound of her voice. He looked up at her. She was so pretty. She was also huge. She weighed over 5000 pounds! He felt tiny beside her at only 400 pounds. But he was only one day old.

The baby enjoyed life on the African savanna. Of course, it helps to be one of the biggest creatures around. And though his little voice didn't quite match his size, no one seemed to notice. Especially the little creatures he played with— the egrets he chased or the tortoise he tickled with the hairs on the tip of his trunk.

hen one day the elephant family smelled something very bad. The baby apologized, but they said it wasn't him this time. No, it was the Takers—heartless animals that just take and take and take, without a care about whom they hurt or what they destroy.

The Takers were after his family's teeth, the long white ivory that most all the elephants had, except the baby.

The Takers charged out of the bush and attacked the baby's family. "Run, little one!" his mom trumpeted.

The baby ran and hid. He waited for his mom to come get him. But she never did.

After days of waiting all alone, the baby heard another family of elephants. He asked them for help. The baby knew of a great river where his family had been before. He thought maybe they were there now, but he needed help finding it.

The leader, Half Tusk, pushed him away. She couldn't be bothered with a lost calf like him.

alf Tusk's sister, Groove, stepped up. She didn't want to leave the baby all by himself. Elephants should stick together. She would take him to the river.

The baby grabbed hold of Groove's tail like he used to do with his mom, and they started on their journey.

Groove decided to call the baby Whispers because of his quiet voice.

fter weeks of travelling, Groove and Whispers saw a fire. Fires are common in Africa, so they weren't afraid. But then the fire was all around them. This wasn't a natural bush fire—it was the Takers!

Before they knew it, Takers surrounded Whispers, their guns raised.

But then Groove burst through the smoke, sounding her trumpet! She rushed in front of Whispers.

The Takers took off running, but not before Whispers heard a loud explosion.

roove and Whispers continued on into the desert, the quickest way to the river. But Groove was struggling. Whispers realized that it wasn't just because she wasn't getting enough water. No, Groove was badly hurt. The explosion had been a gunshot!

Finally, Groove couldn't go on anymore. She told Whispers to go for help.

Whispers tried to find help, but eventually he collapsed too, totally exhausted.

For days, Whispers lay there. Then he heard a familiar call—Half Tusk! The herd had found him. He was saved!

Whispers led Half Tusk back to where Groove lay in the hot sun. As they walked, they flapped their ears to keep themselves cool.

Then they saw her. Half Tusk told Groove how sorry she was for being so strict. She had always loved her.

Whispers was devastated. Groove was dying from a bullet meant for him.

Groove touched his trunk with hers. She didn't like him thinking that way. She was proud to have saved his life.

ut Whispers was still sad. Without Groove, he had no one. He was all alone.

Half Tusk stepped forward. From now on, Whispers would always have a place in her herd. He would never be alone again.

With her family around her, Groove drew her last breath.

Whispers began to run. He ran to hide his sadness and to cover his pain.

Half Tusk led the herd behind him.

After weeks of dusty traveling, Whispers put his trunk up. He smelled water! There it was—the great river.

All the elephants charged into the cool water. They sucked the water up their trunks and blew it into their mouths. It tasted so good!

Suddenly, Whispers saw them again . . . the TAKERS!!

Half Tusk led the herd out of the water and back into the forest to hide. But Half Tusk's daughter, Precious, was stuck at the river's edge!

Whispers heard her calls, and turned back. He dived into the water and pushed her out. Precious ran for the trees.

Instead of following her, Whispers turned to the Takers. Bullets flew past his head.

Whispers was only four feet high, but in his heart he was three times that size. He dipped his head and took a deep breath. Then he raised his trunk and blasted a trumpet louder than any of the Takers had ever heard before.

The Takers looked at Whispers and he looked at them. Neither moved.

ne look at the brave little elephant made the Takers think about what they were doing. They were ruining the world for all the creatures living in it—forever! Finally, they put down their guns.

As the Takers walked away, Whispers thought he saw shame in their eyes. But he knew you could never tell what some animals were thinking.

And all the elephants raised

their trunks up high for Whispers.